SALLY GRINDLEY

has written over 80 children's picture-books
and has just completed her first children's novel.
Her recent books include *Shhh!* and *Why is the Sky Blue?* (both Hodder, 2000),
A New Room for William (Bloomsbury, 2000), *The Giant Postman*
(Kingfisher, 2001) and *Little Elephant Thunderfoot* (Orchard, 2002).
She has been shortlisted four times for the Smarties Prize, has won
the Children's Book Award and one of her books has been
included among the Best Books for Babies.

KARIN LITTLEWOOD'S

highly-acclaimed work includes *Ellie and the Butterfly Kitten*,
shortlisted for the Children's Book Award 2001, *Swallow Journey*,
nominated for the Kate Greenaway Med
and *Chanda and the Mirror of Moonlight*, nom
English Association 4 –11 Awards 2002 and for the Kate
Her first book for Frances Lincoln was Mary 1
The Colour of Home, awarded a WOW award by the
National Literacy Association in 2003.
Also in 2003, Karin donated several illustrations to Frances Lincoln's
anthology *Lines in the Sand: New writings on War and Peace*,
in aid of UNICEF's appeal for the children of Iraq.

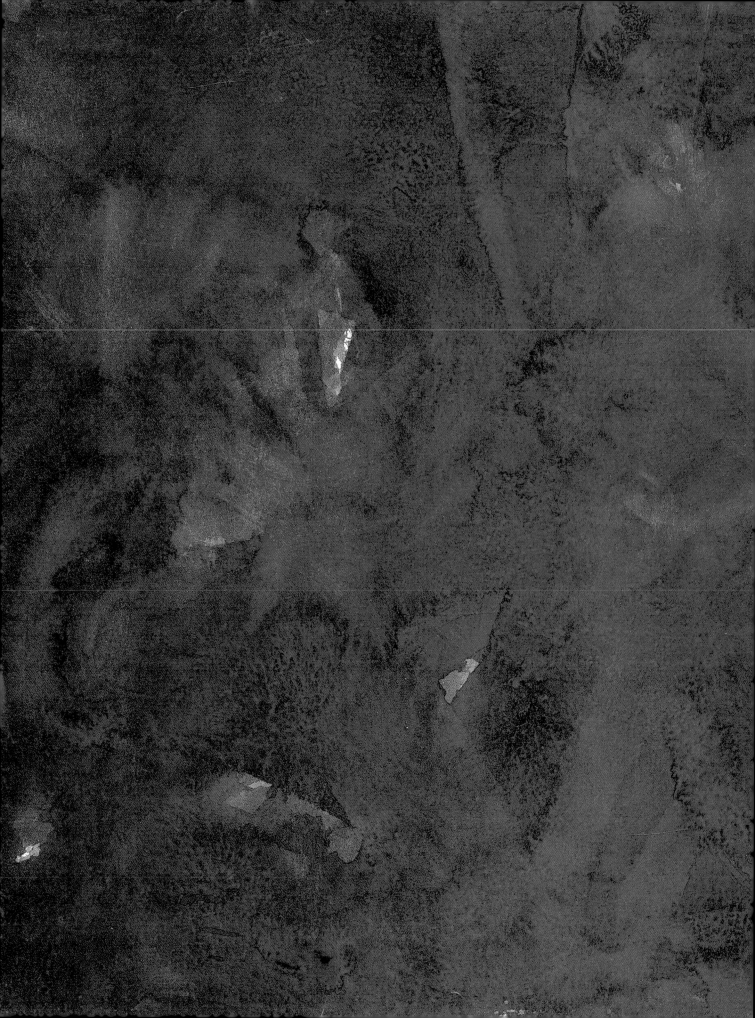

For Arthur – K.L.

First published in Great Britain in 2003 by Frances Lincoln Limited, 4 Torriano Mews

Torriano Avenue, London NW5 2RZ

www.franceslincoln.com

Distributed in the USA by Publishers Group West

First paperback edition 2005

British Library Cataloguing in Publication Data available on request

ISBN 1-84507-137-9

Set in Minion

Printed in Singapore

1 3 5 7 9 8 6 4 2

Home for Christmas

Sally Grindley

Illustrated by Karin Littlewood

FRANCES LINCOLN CHILDREN'S BOOKS

The boy was woken, as he was every morning, by the sounds of cattle shifting anxiously in their stalls. It was another hour until milking time, but they were ready now. He pushed his straw bedding aside and scrambled to his feet. He must be gone before anyone came to tend them. He filled a cup with fresh milk and drank thirstily, patted the animals farewell, then slipped out through the stable door.

The racket and stench of the market spread to every quarter of the town and dragged people from their sleep. Lanterns began to glow from deep inside houses, while voices spilled out through the windows. As the boy hurried along the empty streets towards the market, he wondered what it would be like to wake up in a house with a family.

When he reached the market, the noise was ear-splitting.
Cattle bellowing, hens squawking, sheep bleating,
donkeys braying, men whistling, crates being scraped
along the ground – all jumbled up with an air
of excitement that had grown throughout the week.

"Get to it, lad," shouted a merchant. "The town's full.
We'll be run off our feet today."

The boy picked up a brush and began grooming
the animals. He spoke to them gently, sensing fear
in their wild eyes and whipping tails. Their stale breath
made him choke as it swelled in the cold morning air.

It wasn't long before crowds of people began to arrive at the market. They pushed and jostled, they chattered and laughed, they haggled and demanded. None of them paid any attention to the boy who emptied baskets of fish on to tables and swept the ground around them.

All day he fetched and carried and cleaned, stopping only to bolt down a hunk of bread and cheese and a bowl of thick soup.

And then, as the last few people left in the dull evening light,
the boy noticed a man leading a woman on a donkey.
She looked so weary, the boy felt sorry for her, even though
he was dropping with exhaustion himself.

"Have you something to drink for my wife?" the man asked.

"Too late, mate – we're finished for the day," someone shouted.

The man didn't protest. He turned to go, and the boy felt
ashamed of his workfellow.

The streets were bustling with people when the boy
walked home. The business of the day was over,
and now they were enjoying themselves with family
and friends before travelling back to their own
homes. The boy wished he could join in, but no one
even noticed him as he slipped quietly by.

When he reached the stable, he crept inside, greeted the animals one by one, then wrapped himself up in his straw bedding and quickly fell asleep.

He was woken by the sound of the door opening and whispering voices. His heart beat fast. He listened hard as the door closed again. Had someone discovered his secret hideaway?

A sudden crash of thunder shook the stable. The animals
bellowed in panic. A flash of lightning lit up the stalls.
For a brief second, the boy saw the gaunt face of the woman
he had seen earlier, before it went dark again.

The storm raged on, each clap of thunder more
terrifying than the last. The boy was too frightened
to move. He thought he heard a baby cry,
but he wasn't sure. Then it went very quiet.

The lightning had stopped, but the stable was strangely bright. The boy did not dare to move for a while. Then he peered out from under the straw. Through the gap above the door, a blazing star spilled its light down on to a scene that made him gasp.

The woman was sitting on a low stool, the man standing by her side. In a manger before them lay a tiny baby, surrounded by the animals of the stable. The boy watched from the shadows, fearful that someone would send him away.

Suddenly the man said, "Don't be afraid. We have shared your home: come and share our joy."

The boy crept out from his hiding-place, blinking
in the bright light. Then he took his cup, filled
it with milk and held it out for the woman
to drink. She smiled as he knelt beside her.
"Hold his hand," she said. The boy took
the baby's hand, and as he held it, a feeling
of warmth settled inside him.

During the rest of that long night, visitors came
and left gifts for the baby. Poor shepherds
and wealthy wise men knelt down before him.

The boy looked on wide-eyed. As the hours passed
and the feeling of warmth grew, he knew at last
what it felt like to belong.

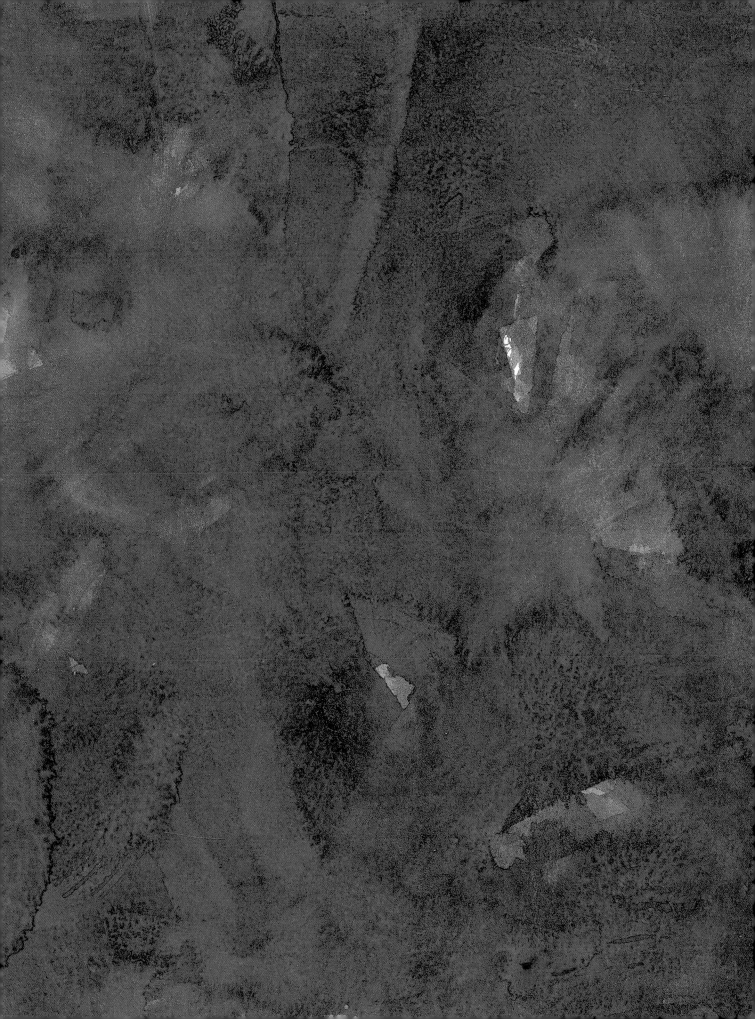